ORCHARD BOOKS
Carmelite House
50 Victoria Embankment
London EC4Y 0DZ

First published as SIDESWIPE VERSUS THUNDERHOOF in 2015 in the
United States by Little, Brown and Company

This edition published by Orchard Books in 2016

A CIP catalogue record for this book is available
from the British Library.

ISBN 978 1 40834 383 8

1 3 5 7 9 10 8 6 4 2

Printed in Great Britain

Orchard Books
An imprint of Hachette Children's Group
Part of The Watts Publishing Group Limited
An Hachette UK Company
www.hachette.co.uk

DECEPTICON ATTACK

BY JOHN SAZAKLIS

ORCHARD

MEET THE TEAM:

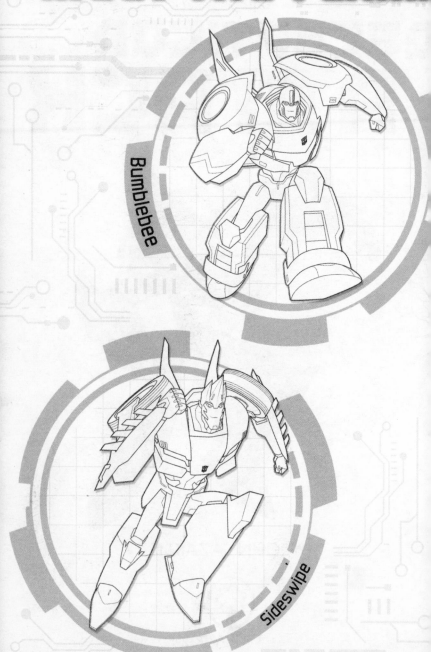

Bumblebee

Sideswipe

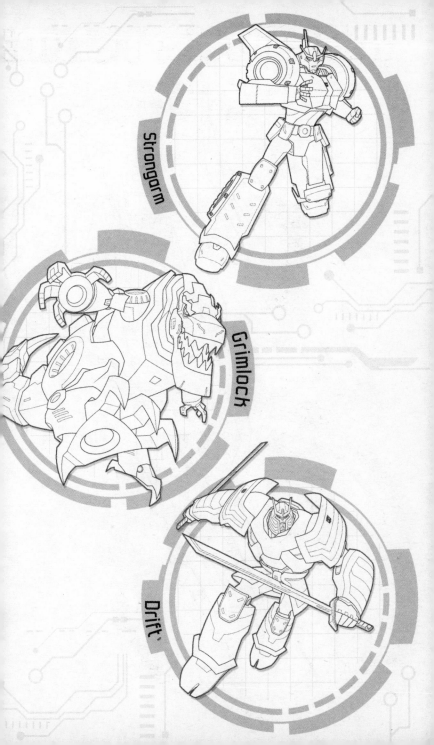

Strongarm

Grimlock

Drift

CONTENTS

FLICK TO SCROLL

STATUS REPORT: A prison ship from the planet Cybertron has crashed on Earth, and deadly robot criminals – the Decepticons – have escaped.

It's up to a team of Autobots to find them and get them back into stasis. Lieutenant Bumblebee, rebellious Sideswipe and police trainee Strongarm have taken the Groundbridge from Cybertron to Earth to track them down.

Along with bounty hunter Drift, reformed Decepticon Grimlock, and the malfunctioning pilot of the ship, Fixit, as well as the two humans who own the scrapyard where the ship crashed, Russell Clay and his dad, Denny, the robots in disguise must find the Decepticons, before they destroy the entire world ...

CHAPTER ONE

ON THE OUTSKIRTS OF CROWN City, two vehicles were racing on a long, secluded stretch of road. One was a cool red sports car, zooming far beyond the legal speed limit. The other, trailing behind, was a blue-and-white police car. Both were more than met the eye. They were really robots in disguise!

The red sports car was Sideswipe, a fast-talking, fun-loving Autobot from the planet Cybertron. Strongarm, the police car, was a young cadet from the Cybertronian Police Force. Both Autobots were members of an elite team that kept Earth safe from some terrible robots known as Decepticons.

"Aw, yeah!" cheered Sideswipe, as the wind rushed past him. "This sure beats sitting around the scrapyard."

"Slow down!" ordered Strongarm.

But the hot-headed Autobot ignored the police-bot's command and picked up more speed.

Sideswipe and Strongarm were always fighting. Sideswipe thought Strongarm was far too serious and hung up on the rules. Strongarm found Sideswipe's disregard for authority extremely annoying.

The red sports car blasted his radio speakers, filling the air with an ear-splitting heavy metal song.

"What an assault on the audio receptors!" Strongarm cried.

"Catch me if you can!" Sideswipe replied. "Or else, eat my dust!"

Sideswipe's tyres kicked up a cloud of dirt as he raced off even faster down the road.

The dust cloud enveloped Strongarm, but she didn't waver in her course.

"You want to play dirty, Sideswipe? Fine by me," she said. "Eat *this*!"

In an instant, Strongarm shifted from her vehicle mode into her robot form. She somersaulted in the air and landed right on top of Sideswipe.

THUD!

"Tag, you're it!" she exclaimed.

"Hey, watch the paint job!" Sideswipe cried. "OK, let's see how strong you really are!"

The sports car swerved quickly to the left and then veered hard to the right.

Strongarm kept her grip as well as her cool.

"Is that the best you've got?" she taunted. "At the academy, we were taught to expect the unexpected."

"Well, we're making an *unexpected* stop," Sideswipe said. "And this is where *you* get off!"

The Autobot slammed on his brakes, and his tyres squealed against the gravel.

SCREEEEE!

Strongarm hurtled forwards and landed on the road in front of Sideswipe.

SLAM!

"Oof!" said Strongarm.

Changing from his vehicle mode into

his robot form, Sideswipe gave Strongarm a hand and helped her off the ground.

"Are you OK?" he asked.

"My ego is more bruised than anything else. I should have heeded my own advice," replied Strongarm.

At that moment, the two Autobots felt a low rumble under their feet. There was another vehicle heading their way.

"Speaking of the unexpected, who is that?" Sideswipe asked.

Strongarm focused her ocular sockets on the approaching object. "It appears to be a human inside a regulation pick-up truck. Probably a local produce supplier. Quick, we must maintain our cover!"

In the blink of an eye, Strongarm and Sideswipe changed back into vehicle form.

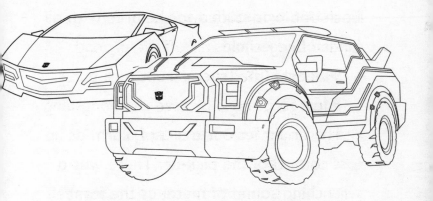

They parked by the side of the road as the farmer's truck approached them.

"Too bad," Sideswipe said. "I was kind of hoping it would be a Decepticon, you know? I'm all revved up and ready for action!"

"Throttle back, tough-bot," Strongarm told him.

The two Autobots remained silent as the pick-up passed by. The bed of the truck was piled high with crates.

Each one was stuffed to the brim with all kinds of vegetables.

Suddenly, the truck's front tyre burst.

BAM!

The driver let out a cry of alarm as he lost control of the pick-up. There was a wrenching sound of metal as the front tyres popped off their axles. The crates on the bed of the truck teetered and tottered while the vehicle swerved from side to side.

"Whoa!" exclaimed Sideswipe. "Who ordered the tossed salad?"

In the distance, a lorry was travelling down the same road in the opposite direction.

"By the Allspark! Those two vehicles are going to collide!" Strongarm cried.

"We have to intervene."

"Well, I wanted excitement," Sideswipe replied. "So let's rock and roll!"

CHAPTER TWO

THE AUTOBOTS RUSHED AFTER THE
runaway truck.

ZOOOOM!

Within seconds, the two heroes
surrounded the pick-up. Strongarm pulled
up close to its right side. The frightened
farmer saw the police cruiser and calmed
down. He gripped the steering wheel and
shouted, "Help me!"

As the pick-up skidded to the left,
Sideswipe was there to keep it steady.
He winced as the truck scraped against
him. There was a shower of sparks as
metal ground against metal.

SKRRRRRRUNCH!

"Mind the paint!" Sideswipe groaned.

"Focus on the big picture," replied Strongarm.

Together, the tenacious team-mates tried to guide the pick-up on to a safe path while helping decrease its speed. Unfortunately, the driver of the oncoming lorry was unaware of the danger that lay ahead.

"That other vehicle isn't slowing down, Sideswipe," Strongarm stated. "I'll need you to take the lead here!"

"Aye, aye, captain!" Sideswipe replied.

The Autobots peeled away from the pick-up and sped past it. Sideswipe went in front and slowed down until his rear bumper touched the truck's bonnet. Then he put on his brakes, bringing both himself and the pick-up to a stop.

Strongarm continued her course, turning on her siren and flashing lights to capture the driver's attention. As the oncoming vehicle careened closer, she realised it was a petrol tanker! If it crashed, it would explode!

"Oh, scrud!" she exclaimed.

The lorry was much closer now but, as he saw the police car, the driver slammed on his brakes. The tyres squealed and screeched on the road. The air filled with dust and the acrid smell of burning rubber, but the truck continued to barrel toward Strongarm — its massive size and weight pushing it forwards.

Thinking quickly, the Autobot turned, bringing her side right next to the truck.

She braced herself for the impact as Sideswipe watched in horror.

"Strongarm … NO!" he yelled.

SCREEEEEEEEEEECH!

The lorry's brakes emitted an ear-piercing squeal as the vehicle ground to a halt.

Then there was silence.

Sideswipe peered through the cloud of dust anxiously. When the dust finally settled, he realised that the lorry had stopped just inches away from Strongarm. But the police car was still in one piece!

Before either Autobot could react, the farmer leaned out of the pick-up window and shouted, "Thank you so much, whoever you are!"

Then he climbed out of the pick-up and walked over to Sideswipe. He tried to peek inside the tinted windows.

BEEP! BEEP!

Strongarm honked her horn, distracting the farmer.

Sideswipe revved his engine and drove around the pick-up and on to the road. Strongarm followed close behind.

The driver of the petrol lorry and the bewildered farmer watched as the mysterious sports car and police car disappeared towards the horizon.

What had started as a friendly competition had nearly ended in disaster. Sideswipe was relieved that Strongarm was unharmed – but he would rather not admit it to her.

After a long while, Strongarm broke the silence. "You know, we kinda work well together," she said.

"Yeah, you're right," Sideswipe replied. "But if you tell anyone back at the base that I said that, I'll deny it! I have a reputation to uphold."

"Deal," Strongarm said, with a laugh.

The Autobots returned to the scrapyard and rolled up through two aisles of junk. There, they switched from their vehicle modes into their robot forms.

The Crown City scrapyard was the Autobots' new command centre on Earth. It belonged to Denny Clay and his twelve-year-old son, Russell.

The two humans had befriended the bots after they literally crash-landed into their lives some time ago. They also helped the Autobots to track down and capture Decepticon fugitives, who were loose on Earth.

"Welcome back, bots!" said a friendly voice as they arrived in the scrapyard.

It belonged to Bumblebee – Sideswipe and Strongarm's determined and kind-hearted team leader. Bumblebee was the lieutenant of the police force back on Cybertron. Now he was in charge of this ragtag bunch of robots that were sometimes more trouble than a dozen Decepticons.

"I hope that exercise helped bring you closer to working together," he said.

"Too close for comfort, if you ask me," Sideswipe said, looking at the scratches on his plating.

"Sideswipe shows great potential, Lieutenant," Strongarm said to Bumblebee. "He just needs to be a little bit more serious."

"If I get any more serious I'll suffer from brain rust," Sideswipe said. "Or worse … I'll turn into you!"

"Keep your optics on the prize, guys," Bumblebee interrupted. "The next training exercise will be centred on the use of our weapons. You know that they are powerful energy weapons that manifest whatever we need in battle through sheer thought or will. That's where your focus counts!"

At that moment, Denny and Russell Clay appeared. Denny let out a long whistle.

"Whoa, Sideswipe, what happened to your side?" he asked. "You really got that authentic 'battle damage' thing going on!"

"Yeah, you look like you went ten rounds with Thunderhoof in the Rumbledome!" Russell added.

"Thunderhoof?" Sideswipe exclaimed, thinking about the huge, elk-like Decepticon that they'd battled once before. "That bunch of rubble doesn't stand a chance against me! He'd better look out! Why, I'll turn him into scrap metal the next time I see him!"

"Quit blowing exhaust," Strongarm chided. "We all know that Thunderhoof is a very dangerous Decepticon. And now that he's loose on Earth *and* he's teamed up with Steeljaw, well, it's enough to give me nightmares for the next ten cycles!"

"Luckily, Thunderhoof, Steeljaw and the rest of the gang have been keeping a low profile," Bumblebee said. "And, speaking of that, what really happened to you?"

Sideswipe smiled. "We just had to intervene and help some civilians in trouble. It was no biggie."

Bumblebee's optics went wide and he gasped out loud.

"You did what?" he exclaimed. "By the Allspark!"

"Relax, Bee," Sideswipe said, with a shrug. "Nothing happened. Nobody saw. We stayed incognito the whole time!"

Bumblebee always worried about keeping the Autobots' presence on Earth hidden from humans, apart from Denny and Russell.

"I've got some touch-up paint," Denny offered to Sideswipe. "We can fix those scratches by buffing the plating out, then wax it up and make you brand-new."

"Sounds good to me," Sideswipe said. "Thanks!"

"Change of plan, team," Bumblebee said. "I just got a message from the command centre: intruder alert!"

CHAPTER THREE

IN RAPID SUCCESSION, BUMBLEBEE
and his team shifted from their bot
modes into vehicles. Strongarm took
Denny as her passenger, and Sideswipe
scooped up Russell.

Together, they raced towards the
command centre – a part of the
scrapyard that had become their new
base of operations.

Two more members of Team Bee were
intently watching the computer screen.
They were the smallest and biggest bots
at the yard.

The little one was Fixit. This mini-con
had been the pilot of the prison transport
ship *Alchemor* – the same ship that had

crashed to Earth and let loose the
countless Decepticon criminals. Now
he served as the resident handy-bot
and lookout.

The big bot was Grimlock. He was a
dinobot and former Decepticon who had
defected to the Autobots. He wasn't
really a bad bot – he was just
misunderstood.

"Intruder dessert ... avert ... alert!"
Fixit cried.

The crash had left Fixit with a slight
speech malfunction. After a quick check,
he fixed himself once again. "I've
prepared all the defence systems. Shall
I activate them?"

The Autobots changed back into bots
and crowded around the mini-con.

"Not just yet," Bumblebee replied. "Allow me to get a closer look."

The lieutenant studied the screen and found three individuals lurking around the perimeter of the scrapyard. One of them was wearing glasses and another had long black hair. The tallest one wore a T-shirt covered with graffiti pictures and had a shaved head.

"Hmm. They appear to be battle-ravaged," Bumblebee stated. "The clothing of one of them is marked with curious and indecipherable symbols. If we scan them into the holo-scroll, we can find out if they are a threat or not."

"They could be the human versions of Decepticons," Sideswipe joked. "They look like they might be bad guys."

Bumblebee shot a stern look at Sideswipe.

"These beings do indeed look unsavoury," Strongarm agreed.

"They don't look so bad to me," said Grimlock. "Maybe they're nice?"

Bumblebee thought for a moment.

The dinobot had a point.

"Grimlock is right," he said. "We shouldn't be so quick to judge. After all, appearances can be deceiving."

Denny let out a belly laugh, startling the group. "You guys should know not to judge things by how they look! Do I need to remind you that you're all robots in disguise?"

Russell pushed his way up towards the screen.

"I know them," he said, with a scowl.

"What are they?" Strongarm asked.

"They're teenagers. And they're my classmates," Russell said with a sigh.

A wave of disbelief passed through the Autobots.

"They're the biggest kids in my year

and they think they rule the school,"
Russell told them.

"Ha!" Strongarm scoffed. "They
wouldn't last a day in the academy."

Fixit fidgeted nervously. "Best not to
take any chimps ... champs ... chances!"
the mini-con stammered.

"The little bot is right! Time for an
interrogation!" Sideswipe shouted
gleefully.

"Hey, I give the orders around here,
remember?" Bumblebee interupted.
"Fixit, stand down. They are civilians."

Bumblebee turned to Sideswipe.
"When I asked you to be a bigger part
of the team, I didn't intend for you to
skip the line straight to leader."

"What can I say, Bee?" Sideswipe

grinned. "I'm an overachiever."

Bumblebee couldn't help smiling in spite of himself.

"Maybe they're customers," Denny said hopefully.

Bumblebee nodded. "Come on, Autobots, we should get out of the way and let Denny and Russell conduct their business as usual."

The bots shifted into their vehicle modes and pulled into empty parking spaces in a small car park full of used cars. Fixit and Grimlock, who didn't have vehicle modes, couldn't hide as easily. Fixit ducked under a large rubbish bin, and Grimlock tried to look as inconspicuous as a huge metal dinosaur could, by freezing in place.

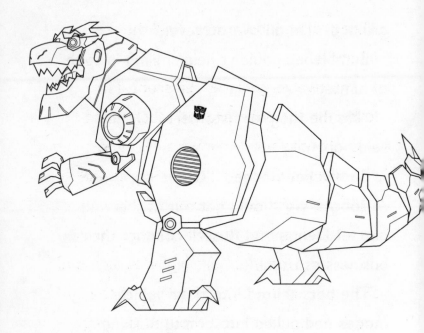

The humans hurried towards the front entrance of the scrapyard.

"This'll be a blast and a half, Rusty," Denny said to his son. "I've never met any of your school friends before."

"It's Russell, Dad. And they're not my friends," Russell said, correcting his father.

"They're my classmates. And they're all idiots."

The twelve-year-old fell silent. His father hadn't been around much when he was growing up. Now, with his mum travelling in Europe, Russell was spending a lot more time with his dad.

In the distance, the three teens climbed on to a rusted and bent highway sign and slid down into another clearing in the yard. They yelled and shouted as they saw all the stuff in the scrapyard.

"Those kids could get hurt doing that," Denny said.

Russell rolled his eyes. "Stay here, Dad. Let me handle this."

Russell walked over to his classmates. The tallest one noticed him first.

"Hey, Joey! Johnny! Look who it is!"

Joey, the red-haired teen with glasses, squinted at Russell and sneered.

"Well, if it isn't little *Rusty* Clay," he said.

"It's Russell," the boy replied.

Johnny, the black-haired kid, ambled over, wiping dirt off his ripped jeans.

"From the looks of this place, we should call him *Dusty* Clay! Ha!"

"Nice one, Johnny," Joey said. "Didja hear that, Steve? Dusty Clay! Ha!

The two friends high-fived each other.

Steve, the tall one with the graffiti top and shaved head, stepped up and looked down at Russell.

"What brings you to our new hang-out, Dusty?" he asked.

"Hate to break it to you, Stevie, but it's *my* hang-out," Russell replied.

Steve blinked in surprise.

"Is that so, small fry?" he taunted. "What if I say it's mine now?"

He shoved Russell to the ground.

A deep voice boomed out from behind the boys. "You're welcome to have it if you want to pay the rent, wise guy!"

"Who you callin' wise—" Steve spun around and came face to face with Denny.

Russell's dad forced a smile.

"I'm Denny Clay," he said. "I'm Russell's father and this is our property," Denny continued. "Can I help you?"

Steve puffed out his chest and took in the surroundings.

"You live in a junkyard? That's lame."

"Actually, it's a vintage salvage depot for the discriminating nostalgist," Denny told him.

Steve, Joey and Johnny exchanged looks. Johnny scratched his head.

"I think you need to use smaller words, Dad," Russell said, getting up off the ground.

Denny stood by his son, "So, unless you're here to make a purchase, I'm going to have to ask you to leave."

Steve cleared his throat and spat on the dirt.

"Let's go, guys," he said to his friends. "This place sucks, anyway."

As the three teens turned to walk away, Joey stopped in his tracks. He ran over to the left side of the yard and readjusted his glasses.

"Whoa!" he shouted. "Maybe this place doesn't suck after all. Look!"

Joey pointed to something in the distance. Steve and Johnny went over to him while Denny and Russell followed his gaze.

"Whoa!" Johnny repeated. "That's so awesome."

At that moment, Denny and Russell realised what the teenagers were gawking at, but it was too late. The secret was out ...

"Oh no," they cried. "Grimlock!"

CHAPTER FOUR

RUSSELL AND DENNY RACED AFTER Steve, Joey and Johnny. The three teens clamoured around the dinobot and stared in awe.

"Check it out, dude. That thing is amazing!" Joey shouted.

"What is it?" Johnny asked.

"Oh, that?" Russell said nonchalantly. "That is a leftover prop from a Japanese monster movie. No big deal, really."

Steve walked around Grimlock, inspecting him from top to bottom.

"Did you say 'Japanese monster movie'?" he asked. "The correct term is *kaiju*, and I've seen each one twice. This guy isn't in any of them."

"Are you sure?" Russell asked, trying to remain calm.

"I'm positive," Steve sneered. "I take my monster movies very seriously."

Suddenly, a voice echoed out from inside a nearby rubbish bin.

"*Kaiju* – Japanese word that translates to 'strange creature'," Fixit said.

Steve whirled around in confusion.

"What did you say?" he asked Denny.

Russell panicked and looked at his dad.

"I picked this strange creature up when I was in Japan," Denny said quickly. "It was made in a little village named Cybertron."

"Cyber-what?" said Joey.

"That's definitely not a real place," added Johnny.

"Oh, it is," Denny continued. "But it's so small it's not even on the map. Good luck finding it!"

"Whatever, garbage man." Steve scowled.

Joey walked around Grimlock this time.

"Actually, he looks more like a dinosaur," the bespectacled boy observed.

"Aw, yeah," said Johnny. "Like from one of those movies about a theme park where humans clone dinosaurs and they escape and start eating people. I love that stuff!"

"This one looks more fake," Joey said.

Grimlock narrowed his optic sensors in anger.

Steve kicked the dinobot with his steel-toed boots.

CLANG!
CLANG!

Grimlock tried really hard not to laugh – the kicks tickled!

"Hmm. Feels fake, too," said Steve.

All of a sudden, Grimlock caught a glimpse of the graffiti on Steve's T-shirt. It was of a cat wearing an astronaut suit.

The dinobot had an irrational fear of felines, and a space cat was especially horrifying!

Suddenly Grimlock roared in fear, waving his arms and stomping his feet.

"SPACE CAT! AAAARGH!"

Steve let out a high-pitched scream and fell on his bum.

"Who turned it on?" he shrieked, as Grimlock continued to flail in fear.

The terrified teen jumped up and turned to run, but he bumped into Joey and knocked the redhead's glasses off – just in time for Johnny to tumble over Joey and trip Steve backwards into an empty refrigerator.

THUMP!

THUD!

"You break it, you buy it," said Russell, with a laugh.

Denny quickly calmed Grimlock down and he froze in place again.

Joey and Johnny lifted Steve out of the fridge, and they ran into the car park.

"You'd better watch your back, junkboy," Steve threatened.

He leaned on the bonnet of a nearby red sports car to catch his breath.

"I think you should watch *your* back," Russell replied.

Suddenly, the car's lights turned on and the horn blared, scaring the teens again.

Steve had leaned on Sideswipe!

The Autobot revved his engine.

VRROOM! VRROOM!

"Gah!" Johnny screamed. "This is just like that movie where a guy's car comes to life and starts killing people. That car was red, too!"

Following Sideswipe's cue, Bumblebee and Strongarm turned on their lights and revved their engines, too.

"I think this place is haunted," Joey said, trembling.

Sideswipe blasted a heavy-metal song from his speakers as loudly as he could.

Steve and his friends covered their ears
and ran out of the scrapyard.

Russell and Denny were laughing so
hard they could barely breathe.

Sideswipe changed back into his bot

mode and joined the humans.

"What a bunch of klutz-o-trons," he remarked.

"Thanks for watching my back," Russell said to the Autobot. "I appreciate it. Those guys are jerks."

"Don't mention it," Sideswipe said.

Bumblebee and Strongarm shifted into their bot modes as well.

"That was a good strategic move you pulled back there," Bumblebee said to Sideswipe. "We backed you up because we trusted your decision. That's how a team works together."

Sideswipe turned away.

"It's hard to tell under that red paint, but I believe he's blushing, sir," Strongarm said, with a smile.

"All right, all right, that's enough,"
Sideswipe yelled. "Isn't there some lesson
Bee should be droning on about?"

Bumblebee brightened.

"Sideswipe, that is another really
excellent idea!"

Strongarm sidled up next to her
lieutenant.

"Yes, more training exercises and
fieldwork," she stated. "That way, we'll
be prepared to fight our Decepticon
enemies."

"I admire your enthusiasm, cadet!"
Bumblebee said. "Let's head to the
command centre."

As Bumblebee and Strongarm walked
away, Sideswipe hung back and leaned
over to Russell.

"Looks like Strongarm may have competition for the position of teacher's bot, heh heh!"

Back at the command centre, Fixit used the holo-scroll to detect any traces of Decepticons. He worked his digits over the keyboard and a three-dimensional map of Crown City appeared.

A bright red dot started blipping in an area southwest of the scrapyard.

"This area has a very high constellation ... constipation ... concentration of Decepticons!" Fixit said. "It is near the Crown City harbour."

"Those look like the docks," Denny said. "There's nothing out there but abandoned warehouses."

"A perfect hiding spot," Bumblebee

replied. "We can use the Groundbridge and catch them by surprise."

He attempted a rallying cry to bring his team of Autobots together. "Let's move it or lose it, team!"

Sideswipe cringed.

"Not bad," he said. "That was your best one yet, Bee!"

"Stop kissing rear bumper!" Strongarm shouted at Sideswipe.

Bumblebee looked out toward the setting sun on the horizon and asked for the guidance of his wise and fallen leader. "Oh, Optimus Prime ... help us keep it together!"

Then he rushed towards the teleportation device.

CHAPTER FIVE

MEANWHILE, ACROSS CROWN CITY
in a more industrial part of town, the
Decepticon called Steeljaw was lying
low in the old steel mill that served as
his hideout.

This cold, calculating criminal had been
the most dangerous Decepticon aboard
the *Alchemor.* Once it had crash-landed,
Steeljaw had made a hasty escape. The
wolf-like warrior had also deactivated the
glowing Decepticon symbol on his body
so he couldn't be tracked.

Steeljaw had soon begun recruiting
fellow Decepticons. With him now were
two of his more cunning cohorts,
Thunderhoof and Underbite.

"Nothing must distract us from annihilating those disgusting Autobots for ever," Steeljaw said. "Then we will be the only powerful beings on this wretched rock!"

"Aw, yeah!" Underbite cheered. "More power gets me pumped!"

The Chompozoid flexed his metallic muscles and then admired himself in a nearby reflective surface. "Let's bring on the bruises, boss!"

"Hrrmph!" Thunderhoof snorted. "Back on Cybertron, I was the boss! Had me my own criminal enterprise. I was running an empire, see?"

Underbite covered his audio receptors. "Not this again," he groaned. "How many times have we gotta hear the same thing? I was running an empire, *wah*, *wah*, *wah*!"

"As many times as it takes for youse guys to get it through your thick heads!" Thunderhoof snapped.

Quick as a flash, Steeljaw leaped through the air and pinned Thunderhoof to the wall.

ROAR!

THUD!

"I'm the boss here, and you should stop talking about being in charge, if you know what's best for you," Steeljaw threatened.

He bared his razor-sharp claws and brought them close to Thunderhoof's snout. They glinted in the light. The elk-like Decepticon trembled, and his antlers rattled against each other.

"Fight! Fight! Fight!" Underbite chanted.

Steeljaw shot him a deadly stare.

Underbite stopped chanting.

"As much as I despise you both, you will prove helpful in achieving my goal – finding the Anti-Spark! With it in my possession, I will bring about unimaginable destruction!"

Steeljaw released Thunderhoof from his vice-like grip.

"Sure thing, Steeljaw," Thunderhoof wheezed. "We'll do things your way ..."

Steeljaw walked away.

Once he was out of earshot,
Thunderhoof added, "… for now."

Then the elkbot trudged towards the
door of the steel mill.

"Where are you going?" Underbite
asked.

"What's it to ya, huh?" Thunderhoof
replied. "I'm gettin' me some fresh air."

"I'll join you," Underbite offered.

"Fine, but keep yer yap shut,"
Thunderhoof said.

Underbite silently followed
Thunderhoof outside. After a few
moments of walking through a dark alley,
the terrible twosome arrived at the dock.

Thunderhoof broke the silence.

"That Steeljaw's got motor oil for

brains if he thinks I can't run an operation," he said. "You wanna know somethin', kid? When I first got to this backwater planet I was runnin' myself a pretty sweet racket."

"What did you do?" Underbite asked.

"You ain't gonna believe this," Thunderhoof said, with a smile. "I convinced a buncha local yokels to help me build a Groundbridge! Made 'em think I was this legendary monster givin' out orders. Called myself 'The Kospego'."

"What's a Kospego?"

"Who gives a scrap? You had to see these fellas runnin' around callin' themselves 'antler-heads' or somethin'!" Thunderhoof pointed at his own antlers and doubled over with laughter.

"So, what happened next?" Underbite asked eagerly.

"They got me all the stuff I needed to build the bridge, see? Got it all laid out nice for me. Had a workin' portal until these wise-guy Autobots suddenly showed up and then the whole shebang went kaput!"

"Sounds like you had a good thing going," said Underbite.

"Ain't that the truth. And I would have got away with it, too, if it weren't for those meddling bots!" Thunderhoof kicked an empty oil drum right across the dock.

CLANG!

"Hey!" Underbite howled. "That was a perfectly good snack!"

The canine robot bounded over to the
dented oil drum and picked it up. Then he
ripped it in half with his bare paws and
bit down on one of the pieces.

CHOMP!

The bot's body started to shimmer and
grow. Being a Chompozoid meant that
Underbite could grow in size and

strength by eating metal.

"Mmm. It's still got some oil in it for extra flavour!" he said, licking his lips. "You want some?"

"Nah," Thunderhoof replied.

"Good," Underbite said. "All the more for me!"

All of a sudden, there was a loud, clattering commotion from inside the warehouse.

BAM!

BANG!

CLANG!

Underbite stopped eating and sniffed the air.

"Smells like trouble," he said, eating the remains of the oil drum. His body shimmered and grew even more.

"Let's get some eyes on the situation before we step in it," Thunderhoof advised.

The elkbot galloped forwards and leaped high into the air. He landed on the roof of the warehouse and waited for Underbite to climb up the side of the wall.

Together, the Decepticons made their way over to a large skylight and peered into the warehouse. One overhead lamp provided the only light. There was movement within.

Thunderhoof and Underbite could see three figures: two of them were lugging large steel drums along, while the third supervised. There were rows and rows of metal shelves lining the floor of the warehouse. The two figures carrying the drums disappeared behind a large shelf. It was stacked high with several identical steel drums.

"Hmm," Thunderhoof mused. "Seems like we ain't the only game in town. Looks like these players are runnin' a racket of their own."

The remaining figure stepped out of the shadows into the moonlight. Underbite gasped.

"It's a catbot!" he snarled. "Catbots are our sworn enemies! *Grrr!*"

Thunderhoof said, "I think it's time for a hostile takeover. What say we drop in with a little welcome party?"

Underbite nodded his massive head in agreement.

With one big leap, the Decepticons
smashed through the skylight into the
warehouse.

SKEESH!

The catbot's audio receptors perked
up, and she whirled around in time to
see the two Decepticons fall into view.

Her claws extended and her back arched.

"Did we catch you at a bad time?" Thunderhoof sneered.

"You've just crossed this black catbot's path," she hissed. "Which means you're in for some bad luck!"

CHAPTER SIX

JUST AS SUDDENLY, TWO MORE Decepticons came rushing from the other end of the warehouse. One of them was a raticon. The other was a weaselbot.

"What's the glitch, boss?" the weaselbot asked the catbot, twitching his whiskers.

"Seems like we got uninvited guests," squeaked the raticon.

"Boss?" Thunderhoof said, his eyes narrowing. Suddenly the antlered Decepticon changed his tune and laid on the charm. "I was a boss back on Cybertron. Maybe you've heard of me? I'm Thunderhoof."

The catbot lowered her claws.

"I'm Slink," she replied. "And your name don't ring no bell to me."

"You sure about that? I'm a pretty big deal," Thunderhoof said, puffing up his chest importantly.

"Look, moose. You heard the lady," the weaselbot said. "Your name don't ring no bell. So make tracks before we wring you out personally."

The raticon swung his tail from side to side and narrowed his beady little optics.

Thunderhoof gritted his teeth but maintained his cool.

"And who might you be?"

"I'm Sneak," said the weaselbot.

"I'm Snitch," said the raticon.

"And I'm the Devourer of Nuon City!" growled Underbite.

"Underbite!" Thunderhoof scolded. "You ain't helping."

Slink hissed at the Chompozoid.

"Why don'tcha keep that mutt on a leash?" she said.

"That's it, catbot! You're about to lose four of your nine lives!"

Slink stepped back and whistled.

"Boys? Sic 'em!"

In an instant, the two Decepticon lackeys leaped into action, springing towards Underbite. They slammed him backwards, each bot pinning one of his arms to the wall.

"Looks like it's time for me to take out my boys," Underbite grunted. He flexed his bulging biceps and broke free from Snitch and Sneak.

"Meet Thundercruncher!" cried the Chompozoid, as he wound up a right uppercut.

BANG!

Sneak went sailing through the air and crashed into a metal shelving unit.

CLANG!

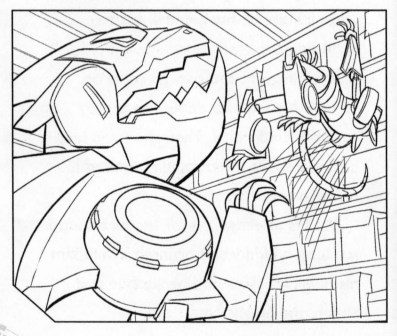

Underbite kissed his right bicep and said, "Thanks, Thundercruncher." Then he turned to face Snitch.

"Meet Boltsmasher!" shouted the Chompozoid, and he swung his left fist at the raticon.

Snitch surprised Underbite and dropped low to the ground. He swung his large tail in an arc and swept the Chompozoid off his feet.

Underbite landed hard.

THUD!

"Keep the introductions to yerself!" Snitch sneered.

At that moment, Sneak recovered and pounced on Underbite. Snitch joined him and the two Decepticons slashed and bashed the big Chompozoid.

"Two bots are better than one!" Sneak cheered.

Underbite lifted each of his opponents by the neck and slammed their heads together.

KLONK!

"They sure are!" he retorted.

Meanwhile, outside the abandoned factory, there was a burst of bright, colourful light that signalled the opening of a portal. Team Bee stepped out of the Groundbridge, and the brightness disappeared as soon as it closed.

Bumblebee surveyed the surroundings. The industrial area was a large maze of tall, concrete buildings. The full moon provided some light, its reflection skittering across the rippling waves of the water beyond the docks.

The stillness allowed Bumblebee's thoughts to catch up with him. His new role as leader was at times uncomfortable and frustrating.

Something shifted along the water's surface and took a familiar shape. Curious, Bumblebee peeked over the side of the dock and looked down to see the reflection of his fallen leader.

"Optimus," he whispered warily, "is that you? Got any advice on how to lead a group with no military training whatsoever? I'm just wingin' it here, and every time I think they've learned how to work together, they start bickering and fall apart."

The reflection rippled but did not disappear. Bumblebee could hear the Prime's voice in his head.

You were once as inexperienced as your team-mates, and yet your limitless potential has surpassed my greatest expectations. I see the same dynamic spark within your team. You are a leader, Bumblebee, and you have made me proud.

Suddenly, the Autobot felt a hand on his shoulder.

"Optimus! Oh, hey, Grimlock," Bumblebee said, embarrassed. "Must've drifted off. Sorry."

"Seems quiet," the dinobot whispered.

"Are we in the right place?"

"Too quiet, if you ask me," Bumblebee replied. "But these are the coordinates Fixit gave us. Let's look around."

The Autobot and his team walked towards the warehouse.

"We should set up a perimeter," Strongarm said.

"Excellent idea, cadet," Bumblebee replied.

"I was just gonna say that!" said Sideswipe.

Strongarm rolled her optics.

"We should enter from the back door," Sideswipe continued. "Catch them by surprise."

"We should drop in from the roof," Strongarm offered. "An aerial view would allow us to acquire the targets faster."

"Both are viable options," Bumblebee replied. "So we'll split up into pairs and double our chances at capturing these criminals."

Suddenly, the warehouse wall erupted in a huge explosion.

KA-BLAM!

Bumblebee, Sideswipe, Strongarm and Grimlock jumped back and shielded themselves from the flying debris.

The large projectile that had caused the explosion now landed on the dock with a ground-shaking thud.

It was their familiar foe Underbite, engaged in a raging battle with two unidentified Decepticons!

WHAM!

Bam!

The Chompozoid grabbed one of the Decepticons by his long tail and whipped him through the gaping hole in the wall. The other Decepticon tackled Underbite from behind, and they both tumbled back into the warehouse.

"Or ..." Grimlock said, peeking in after them, "we find out what's behind door number three!"

CHAPTER SEVEN

TEAM BEE STEALTHILY ENTERED THE warehouse, prepared for anything but the scene that was before them.

While Underbite continued fighting with Snitch and Sneak, Thunderhoof was casually talking with Slink.

"I see you're a fellow entrepreneur," he said, sliding his arm around her.

"Cut the scrap, antler-head," Slink snapped. She wriggled out of Thunderhoof's embrace. "I got here first. Fair and square. If you had marked this territory, I woulda smelled your stench from a mile away!"

"Listen up, sweet-bot, this here is *my* territory," Thunderhoof replied.

"So if youse wanna conduct business 'round these parts, youse play by my rules. I'm the boss! And I get a cut of yer profits."

"Not a chance," Slink snarled.

Thunderhoof snorted loudly, exhaling steam from his snout. "Well, then, I guess we do this the hard way. No more Mr Nice-Bot!" he shouted.

He lunged at Slink and grabbed her.

"Stand down, Thunderhoof!" a booming voice echoed through the warehouse.

The commotion stopped, and all the Decepticons turned to see Bumblebee and his team standing in front of the broken wall, heroically silhouetted against the full moon.

Strongarm had her blaster aimed at the elkbot.

"You're under arrest!" she called.

"Scrud!" cried Snitch. "It's the law-bots!"

"Everybot put your hands where I can see them," Bumblebee ordered. "NOW!"

Thunderhoof raised Slink into the air and used her as a shield. The catbot kicked at her captor, but his grip was just too strong.

"Mine are right here, law-bots," he taunted. "But don't any of youse go makin' no sudden moves or nothin', 'cuz I'll crush her intake valve."

Underbite followed suit and grabbed his opponents in each fist. Snitch and Sneak squirmed and trembled in the massive mitts of the Chompozoid.

Strongarm put Thunderhoof in her sights. "I have a clear shot, Lieutenant," she whispered to Bumblebee.

"Hold back," he replied.

Strongarm lowered her weapon.

"Smart bot," Thunderhoof said. "I'm the boss, see, and this is how things are gonna go down. Me and Underbite are gonna trade youse these here punk junk-bots for a free ride, capiche?"

"None of you are leaving the premises unless it is in a stasis pod," Bumblebee stated firmly.

"Is that so?" the elkbot responded. "How's about we cut a deal? I'll even give youse the friends and family-bot discount."

"What's that?" Grimlock asked.

"You get two Decepticons for the price of one!" Underbite roared.

The Chompozoid hurled Snitch and Sneak directly at the Autobots.

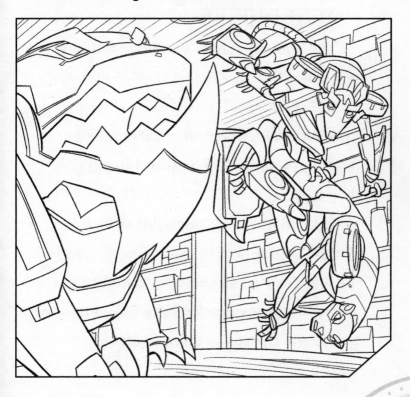

SMASH!

Bumblebee, Grimlock and Strongarm were taken by surprise, but Sideswipe acted swiftly. He shifted into his vehicle mode and rocketed towards Thunderhoof.

VROOOOOM!

The speedy sports car slammed into the elkbot.

BAM!

Slink broke free and somersaulted through the air. The catbot landed on her feet.

Sideswipe struck again, launching Thunderhoof across the room, where he bashed into a tall shelving unit. The shelves tipped over into the next unit, and the next, causing a domino effect.

CLANG!

BANG!

Tin cans, steel drums and metal trays clattered and crashed all around the Cybertronians with a huge crash.

"Who's the boss now?" Sideswipe quipped.

The other Autobots followed Sideswipe's lead and charged into battle.

Rushing toward the dazed Decepticons, Bumblebee and Strongarm confronted Snitch and Sneak.

Bumblebee wielded an energy sword. The blade illuminated the dark warehouse with an iridescent blue glow.

Snitch and Sneak shielded their optics from the blinding light.

"Arms up, Decepticons!" ordered Bumblebee while brandishing the blade.

"We get the point, cop-bot," Snitch said. "Sneak and I are more than happy to oblige. Ain't we, Sneak?"

"Sure thing, Snitch," Sneak replied with a sly grin.

In a flash, the weaselbot lifted his arms up over his head and squirted two pungent puffs of a ghastly green gas at Bumblebee.

FSSSSS!

FSSSSS!

"Drop and roll!" Strongarm shouted, jumping back to avoid the gas.

But it was too late. The Autobot leader caught a whiff of the toxic fumes, and they caused his neuro-sensors to go haywire. He hacked and wheezed and stumbled through the thick cloud.

With one blind swipe, he managed to catch Sneak with the broad side of the energy blade, knocking him back into his buddy Snitch.

CLANG!

Bumblebee finally heeded his cadet's advice, put away his weapon and changed into his vehicle form. He drove out on to the docks and into the cold fresh air.

Sneak watched him go and cackled. "I ain't no business-bot, but that seems like the sweet smell of success to me!"

The weaselbot pumped his fists in the air and gave the raticon a high five.

"You're not getting away that easily," Strongarm said, willing her weapon to become a double-bladed energy sword.

Twirling it with considerable skill,
Strongarm brought one end down on
Snitch.

WHAP!

Then she whirled it over her head and
brought the other end down on Sneak.

WHACK!

Strongarm put down her weapon and
pulled a steel cable off a nearby hook.
The Autobot wrapped it around Sneak,
pinning the weaselbot's limbs at his side.

"On second thought, keep your arms
down!" Strongarm commanded.

Before she could get to Snitch, the
raticon whipped around and hit
Strongarm with his tail.

SMACK!

The Autobot was knocked off her feet.

THUD!

Snitch rushed over to Sneak and started nibbling through the metal coils with his sharp, bucked front teeth.

"I'll have you out in less than a nano-second," Snitch said.

"Less chat, more chew!" Sneak grumbled.

Meanwhile, Thunderhoof pulled himself out from under the heavy fallen shelf. The elkbot was covered in meaty chunks.

"Say, what is this filth?" he asked, brushing himself off.

Slink appeared from the shadows and purred, "It's called pet food. The fellas on this backwards rock use it to feed something called a pet. They all got 'em, and they'd pay their weight in Energon to get their hands on it ... were there a shortage, see?"

Thunderhoof shook his head. "I gotta admit, Slink, ol' gal, that ain't a bad racket at all."

Slink smiled, baring her sharp teeth.

"I'm glad you think so, big fella, 'cuz if you wanna be in my gang, you'll need your own set of whiskers."

With that, Slink scraped Thunderhoof's snout with her claws, leaving matching scratches on either side. The elkbot howled in pain.

"Serves ya right, you slimy slag-heap!" Slink hissed.

Thunderhoof leaped to his feet, but when he reached out to grab Slink, she was gone.

"Come out and fight me, ya scaredy-catbot!" he yelled.

"Mind if I cut in?" said a voice behind Thunderhoof.

The elkbot turned and came into direct contact with Sideswipe's fist.

POW!

"Let's dance!" Sideswipe yelled. He turned on his radio speakers and filled the air with a bass-heavy electronic dance anthem.

Thunderhoof took a swing at the young Autobot, but Sideswipe backflipped out of the way. He hopped on to an upturned shelf and grooved to the music.

The elkbot snorted in disgust and charged at Sideswipe, who stopped Thunderhoof's momentum with a swift kick to the chest.

WHAP!

The Decepticon staggered back, then charged forward again with renewed vigour.

Sideswipe evaded Thunderhoof's strike by leaping around him like a cricket and attacking with a rapid succession of jabs and hooks.

Thunderhoof finally got his bearings and began to expertly block Sideswipe's flurry of punches. In a flash, he grabbed both of the Autobot's hands in his mitts.

"You got some gears in ya, kid, I'll give you that," Thunderhoof said, trying to catch his breath. "Fast with your mouth, faster with your fists. But you gotta use your head once in a while, too!"

The elkbot reared back and brought his antlers crashing down on Sideswipe.

THUNK!

The Autobot crumpled into a heap on the floor. The happy music came to an abrupt stop.

"I could use a bot like you in my gang," Thunderhoof said, standing over Sideswipe. "But first, we gotta remind ya who's boss!"

The Decepticon raised his heavy hoof, preparing to crunch Sideswipe's head into the ground.

BAM!

SMASH!

CRASH!

While the Autobots and Decepticons clashed, Slink quickly and quietly packed a forklift truck with piles of salvageable pet-food cans.

"I better git while the gittin's good!" she said to herself. The catbot scanned the area for her lackeys and spotted them across the room.

Snitch had finally gnawed through the steel cable that had been wrapped around Sneak.

Slink whistled to get their attention.

"Git yer lousy hides over here and help me!" she hissed.

The raticon and weaselbot jumped to attention and bounded over towards their boss.

At the same time, Underbite picked up a supersize tin and looked at the label.

"Power Pup Dog Food," read the Chompozoid out loud. "Lemme try some of this!"

Underbite emptied the contents of the tin on to the ground and crunched the container between his paws. Then he chucked the mashed-up metal into his huge mouth.

CHOMP!

His body shimmered with energy, and he grew a little bigger.

"Mmm! I've got the power!" he snarled. "Who wants some of this?"

"Me!" shouted Grimlock. The dinobot rushed towards the Chompozoid.

"You wanna go one-on-one with the Devourer of Nuon City?" Underbite taunted.

"You're looking at Cybertron's living lob-ball legend, Gridlock Grimlock!" replied the dinobot.

"Bring it on, big guy!" shouted Underbite.

Grimlock shifted from dino to bot mode and picked up an enormous steel drum.

"Catch!" he yelled, and snapped it at the Chompozoid, hoping to knock him down like a bowling pin.

But Underbite ran towards the metal drum, leaped into the air, and caught it close to his chest. Then he ripped it in two and swallowed both pieces in the blink of an eye.

CHOMP!

CHOMP!

GULP!

His body rippled with glowing energy, and he grew a foot taller.

SHOOM!

"Thanks for the boost, bro-bot!"
Underbite said to Grimlock. "I can feel
the power!"

"Uh, maybe that was a bad idea,"
Grimlock gulped.

Underbite laughed.

"Guess it's time to unleash the Dino-Destructo Double Drop!" Grimlock said.

"Let's get ready to rumble!" Underbite shouted.

Grimlock charged Underbite, and the two robots tackled each other to the ground.

CHAPTER EIGHT

MEANWHILE, STRONGARM WAS recovering from Snitch's attack. She looked round and took in the situation.

To her left, Underbite and Grimlock were locked in battle. To her right, Snitch and Sneak were loading a forklift, with Slink in the driver's seat.

Straight ahead, Thunderhoof's humungous hoof hovered over Sideswipe's battered body. Strongarm made her decision. She aimed her plasma cannon and fired two shots.

ZAP!

ZAP!

The first blast caught Thunderhoof in his shoulder and spun him around.

The second blast caught him in the back and sent him tumbling headfirst over his own hooves.

SPLAT!

Strongarm rushed to Sideswipe's side and revived her groggy team-mate.

"Uh … thanks," Sideswipe said as Strongarm helped him off the ground. "Gimme a nanocycle to catch my ball bearings."

"I guess I owed you one, huh?" Strongarm replied. "Now let's regroup and figure out our next plan as a team. We're in over our heads here."

Before the two Autobots could take another step, Thunderhoof appeared behind them.

"Youse are gonna be deactivated—"

BEEP!
BEEP!

Thunderhoof was interrupted by a honking horn. He turned to see Slink zoom by with her henchbots in the loaded forklift.

The elkbot's jaw dropped. "What in the—?"

Strongarm grabbed Sideswipe, and the two Autobots ran away while Thunderhoof was distracted.

"Don't think I'm letting youse make tracks with my goods, Slink!" he shouted. "I'm not lettin' you outta my sight!"

"We'll see about that," the catbot purred. Slink extended her paws and shot bladed claw projectiles. The razor-sharp darts zipped through the air and shattered the lightbulbs in the overhead lamps.

SKEESH!

The warehouse was plunged into darkness.

Just as quickly, Slink shouted, "Get into stealth mode, boys!"

Glowing green lenses popped up over the bandit-bots' optics, giving them all night vision.

"Not only are they nasty, they're nocturnal, too!" Strongarm observed.

She could hear Thunderhoof stomping around blindly and hurling insults at anyone within an audio receptor's reach.

Oblivious to their surroundings, Underbite and Grimlock continued to tussle and clash, until the two titans crashed through a nearby wall.

SMASH!

When they landed on the docks, Grimlock had the upper hand. He was straddling Underbite and pummelling the Chompozoid with both his fists.

POW!

WHAP!

POW!

But then Underbite rolled over and pinned Grimlock to the dock. He bared his sharp jaws and said hungrily, "I've never eaten dinobot before. I wonder if it tastes like chickenbot!"

The Chompozoid lunged forward and
bit into Grimlock's shoulder.

"YOWCH!" yelled Grimlock.

"Someone help!"

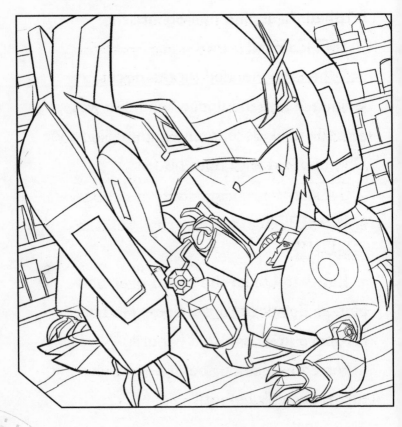

As Underbite lunged for a second bite, he was distracted by the loud screeching sound of burning rubber.

SCREE!

The high-pitched squeal hurt the Chompozoid's sensitive audio receptors, and he covered them with his hands. He looked up to see a yellow sports car speeding around the corner and heading his way – it was Bumblebee!

The Autobot changed into his robot form and rushed towards the brawling bruisers.

"Biting is not a regulated move, according to Rumbledome rules," Bumblebee stated.

"Well, I'm not in the ring now," Underbite growled at Bumblebee.

"So just wait your turn while I make this dinobot extinct!"

Grimlock's optics went wide.

"Tap me out, Bee," he said, rubbing his shoulder. "This game isn't fun any more."

"How about you pick on someone your own size?" Bumblebee replied.

"Who, you?" Underbite sneered down at Bumblebee nastily.

He reached for Bumblebee, but the Autobot sidestepped the Chompozoid and delivered a roundhouse kick.

WHAP!

Underbite reeled back, giving Grimlock an opening to leap up and bring a double-fisted elbow drop raining down on the Chompozoid.

POW!

Bumblebee administered a devastating punch that lifted Underbite into the air.

BAM!

Grimlock finished the four-hit combo with a swift judo chop to the back of the Decepticon's thick neck.

KA-POW!

Underbite hit the wooden planks so hard he splintered them. With his nose stuck inside the dock, the Chompozoid was momentarily down for the count.

With the moonlight streaming into the warehouse, Thunderhoof spotted the shape of the forklift.

"You ain't goin' nowhere," he yelled at Slink. The elkbot's eyes glowed red with anger, and steam billowed out of his snout. Then he flexed, reared back and lifted his hoof. He stomped the ground hard, emitting powerful seismic waves of energy – like an earthquake!

SHOOM!

The concrete rippled and cracked, starting at the foundation and spreading all the way through to the walls. Then the building began to buckle under its own weight.

"The integrity of the entire warehouse is compromised!" Strongarm shouted. "Quick! We have to leave, right now. This place is coming down!"

Sideswipe looked up as the ceiling began to cave in. His optics went wide with horror.

"We better bail before we become a bunch of buried bots!"

CHAPTER NINE

VROOOOOM!

Sideswipe and Strongarm changed modes from bot to vehicle and rushed out of the collapsing warehouse.

BAM!

SMASH!

Iron girders and steel support beams came crashing down into their path. The sports car and police car went weaving in and out of the wreckage until they were finally outside.

The Autobots zoomed towards the docks to find Bumblebee and Grimlock standing over Underbite, who was still knocked out.

"Yo, Bee!" Sideswipe called out. "Burn some rubber, dude. This whole place is falling apart!"

Bumblebee looked down as the dock began to splinter and crack. Chunks of concrete and metal rained down from above them.

Underbite came to and realised the danger around him.

"This is way above my power grade!" he growled, and jumped to his feet. The Chompozoid stumbled towards the empty alley and shouted over his shoulder at the Autobots. "Sayonara, suckers!"

Bumblebee shifted into his vehicle mode as Grimlock stomped away from the warehouse.

The Autobots raced towards the safety of the dock's edge.

Behind them, the last bits of the warehouse finally buckled and collapsed into a humongous heap of debris.

FWOOM!

Then ... silence.

All was quiet once again in the industrial area, where moments earlier a battle had raged between Autobots and Decepticons.

"Well, that mission was a bust," Sideswipe complained. "Literally."

"There must be a way to fix it," Bumblebee said.

"You raft ... rant ... rang?" Fixit asked, radioing in to their audio frequency.

Bumblebee chuckled and said, "I didn't mean you! But since you're there, what have you got?"

"I've picked up the location of our newest Decepticon targets. They are moving north, away from your location. And they are moving fast."

"They sure are some slippery scoundrels," Strongarm stated.

"Is there any sign of Thunderhoof?" Sideswipe asked.

"I'm not getting a reeking ... reeling ... reading," Fixit sputtered.

"Do you think he was buried in the building?" Grimlock asked.

"Good riddance," Sideswipe huffed.

"No, Sideswipe," Bumblebee admonished the hotheaded Autobot.

"We can't disregard any Cybertronian life, even if it's that of a criminal Decepticon. We can only hope to keep Earth safe until we can rehabilitate them."

"Beautifully put, sir," Strongarm said.

"Speaking of," Fixit interrupts, "the fumigates ... fooditives ... fugitives are getting away!"

"Send us the coordinates and we'll pursue immediately," Bumblebee said.

Fixit did so, and the bots revved their motors. Bumblebee summoned another spontaneous rallying cry.

"Let's burn some rubber, bots!"

"Hey, good one," Sideswipe replied.

"I like the way you think!"

As the Autobots sped away, something buried under the rubble of the warehouse began to move. Chunks of rock and dirt shifted to reveal a huge pair of gleaming, metallic antlers.

Soon the rest of Thunderhoof emerged from the debris. His eyes glowed with rage, and smoke billowed from his snout.

"Now I'm really steamed!"

The Autobots drove through the maze-like warehouse district, finally reaching the other end of the harbour and shifting back into their bot modes.

Bumblebee saw Slink, Snitch and Sneak in their forklift driving toward the boats.

"Here's the plan," he said.
"Strongarm and I will go on the
offensive and capture the fugitives.
Sideswipe and Grimlock will stay here
and block them from escaping in case
we fail."

"Roger that, Bee," Sideswipe replied.

Bumblebee and Strongarm sprang
into action, sprinting down the dock
and leaping into the air. Strongarm
whipped out her weapon and created a
crossbow. She fired an arrow at the
topmost steel drum on the lift.

CLANG!

Direct hit!

The drum tipped over and landed in
front of the vehicle, causing Slink to
slam on the brakes.

Bumblebee descended from above, wielding his energy blade. The sword's bright glow illuminated the night sky as Bumblebee used it to slice right through the forklift.

SWISH!

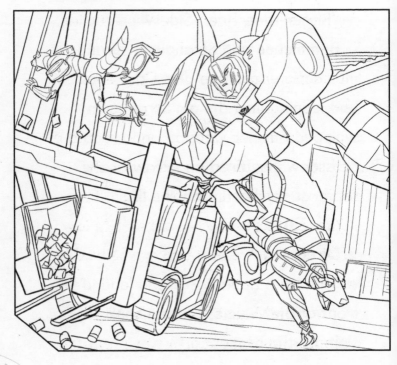

"Jump for yer lives!" Slink shouted.

The Decepticons scattered on to the dock. Their escape vehicle split in half like a chopped melon, its edges smouldering.

"That was close," whined Snitch.

The fugitives hopped to their feet, but they found their path blocked by Strongarm and Bumblebee.

"It's the end of the line, Decepticons. Time to face justice," Strongarm commanded.

"Let's swim fer it!" Sneak shouted.

"Forget about it!" Slink shrieked. "Catbots hate water, remember? Now make yerselves useful and snuff out those law-bots!"

Snitch and Sneak rushed at the Autobots, but Strongarm was prepared.

Her weapon configured itself into a net launcher. Out from the launcher sprang a steel net coursing with electricity. It covered the Decepticons and gave them a jolt.

ZAP!

They slumped to the floor, unconscious.

Strongarm bound their wrists together.

"Curses!" hissed Slink. "If you want something done ... you gotta do it yerself!"

She somersaulted forwards and unleashed her claws, swiping them at Bumblebee. The Autobot raised his blade and deflected the attack. Sparks flew as the opponents clashed and slashed away at each other.

Slink struck again, and Bumblebee parried her thrust.

CLANK!

He sidestepped and brought the hilt of the blade down on to Slink.

THUD!

The Decepticon fell forwards but retaliated with a kick that knocked the weapon from Bumblebee's hands.

"I'm afraid our evening has come to an end," Slink said, and prepared to shoot her claw-darts at the Autobot. "Say goodnight!"

"Ladies first," Bumblebee replied.

He grabbed Slink by her forearm before she could shoot and hurled her over his shoulder. She landed on Snitch and Sneak and was zapped by the net.

ZZAPPK!

"Nice moves, Lieutenant," Strongarm said, with a smile.

Bumblebee thanked her as Sideswipe and Grimlock arrived, upset about missing all the excitement. As they complained, Bumblebee contacted Fixit back at the command centre.

"Fixit? We've got some of the the Decepticons. Whip us up a Groundbridge, will ya?"

The mini-con opened the glowing portal, and the Autobots walked into the light. Grimlock led the way, dragging the snoozing criminals behind him. Then Bumblebee and Strongarm entered. Sideswipe sauntered behind them, bringing up the rear.

Suddenly, the young Autobot was blindsided by a hulking figure and roughly lifted off his feet.

"Oof!"

The other Autobots and the Groundbridge disappeared as Sideswipe hurtled across the docks and landed on a nearby large boat. Dazed and disoriented, the Autobot looked up just in time to see his attacker crashing down on top of him.

"Thunderhoof!" Sideswipe grunted. "Ready for round two?"

The elkbot laughed. "There's that fast mouth runnin' off again. Let's see how much you can say when you're sleepin' with the fishes."

Thunderhoof lifted Sideswipe up over his head, ready to throw him overboard.

Sideswipe scrambled to reach his
weapon. He clumsily dropped the device
and watched it roll across the deck.

"Scrap," he whispered.

"Bon voyage!" Thunderhoof yelled,
and heaved Sideswipe out to sea.

The tough young Autobot grabbed on
to the boat's railing just in time and
slammed into the port side of the ship.
Sideswipe winced, but ignored the pain.
Furious, Thunderhoof searched the boat
for a weapon and discovered a harpoon.

Sideswipe's optics went wide as the
Decepticon advanced with the sharp
implement held up high. The Autobot's
free arm reached out and grabbed
something dangling nearby.

"Guess I'll have to scrape this barnacle
off the boat the old-fashioned way,"
Thunderhoof snorted.

The elkbot raised the harpoon but
before he could move, Sideswipe stuffed a
round life buoy around his antlers.

WHUMP!

"That's enough out of you," Sideswipe quipped. "I make the jokes around here."

The elkbot dropped his weapon and grappled with the flotation device. Sideswipe hoisted himself on to the boat and scurried to his weapon. He was outmatched in pure strength and instead decided to rely on his quick thinking.

After an awkward struggle, Thunderhoof finally ripped the life buoy off his antlers and howled. "AARGH! You'll pay for this!"

"Hey, you were the one who told me to use my head, remember?"

The elkbot smiled. He lowered his head and aimed his antlers at Sideswipe. He charged wildly, intent on spearing the Autobot once and for all.

At the last second, just as Thunderhoof was about to deliver his devastating blow, Sideswipe flipped backwards and grabbed on to the mast.

Thunderhoof's massive size and momentum sent him crashing through the railing.

SPLASH!

The Decepticon plunged into the depths of the Crown City harbour.

Sideswipe hopped down and peeked over the edge. There was no sign of his adversary in the dark, rippling water.

Just as he was about to contact his team-mates, the Groundbridge reappeared.

Bumblebee stepped out and found Sideswipe on the boat. "There you are!

Is this your way of getting out of stasis pod cleaning?"

"Nah, I just had some unfinished business to take care of."

Sideswipe hopped on to the dock. He told Bumblebee what had happened with Thunderhoof.

Bumblebee reacted with surprise. "I'm impressed, Sideswipe! Way to step up your game."

"Hey, I had a good teacher," Swideswipe said, and fist-bumped Bumblebee. "It's gonna be a long walk back to shore for Thunderhoof."

"Yep," Bumblebee replied, looking out over the wide stretch of water. "And we have to be ready to catch him next time. So let's go and recharge."

The two bots headed towards the Groundbridge as the sun began to rise along Crown City's coast.

Bumblebee caught a glimpse of Optimus Prime's reflection in the water, and he was almost convinced that the great Autobot hero was smiling.

"I'm proud of us, too," Bumblebee whispered.

Then the great Autobot leader disappeared in a flash of blinding light.

··· MISSION COMPLETE ···

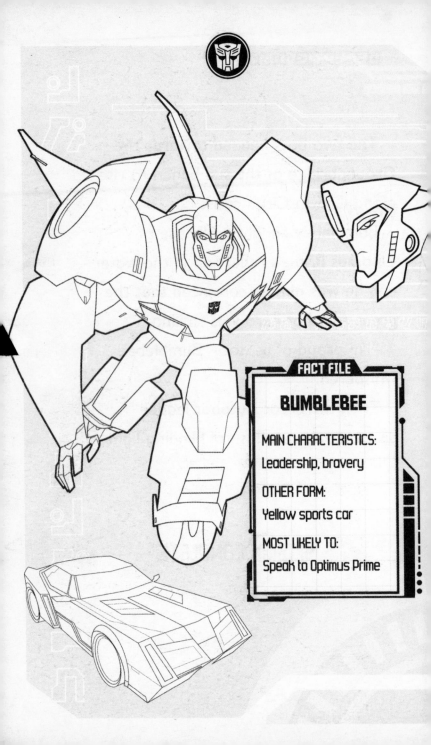

FACT FILE

BUMBLEBEE

MAIN CHARACTERISTICS:
Leadership, bravery

OTHER FORM:
Yellow sports car

MOST LIKELY TO:
Speak to Optimus Prime

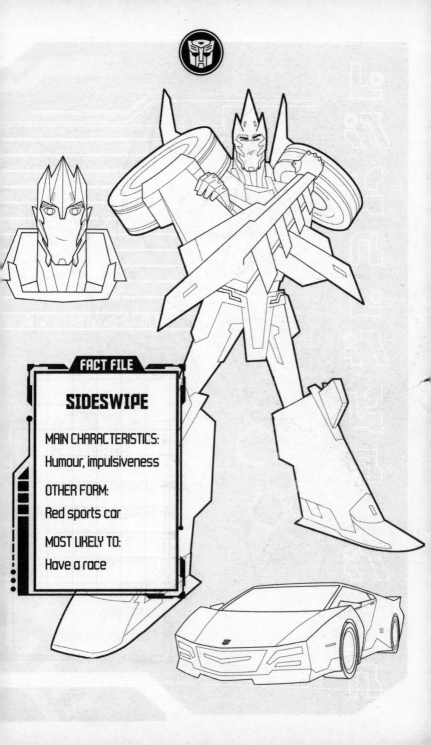

FACT FILE

SIDESWIPE

MAIN CHARACTERISTICS:
Humour, impulsiveness

OTHER FORM:
Red sports car

MOST LIKELY TO:
Have a race

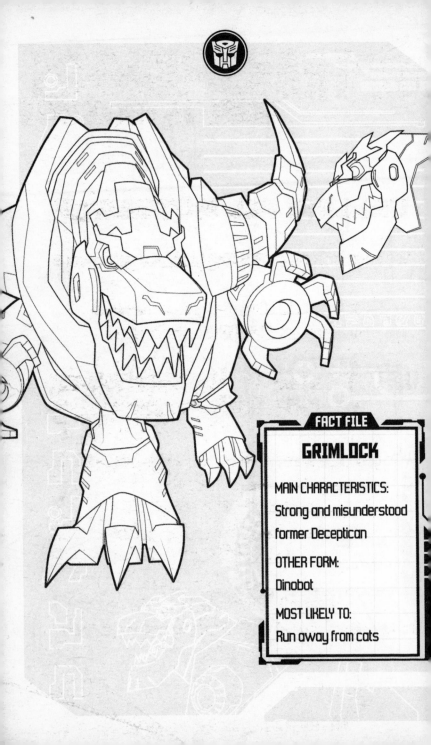

FACT FILE

GRIMLOCK

MAIN CHARACTERISTICS:
Strong and misunderstood
former Deceptican

OTHER FORM:
Dinobot

MOST LIKELY TO:
Run away from cats

CALLING ALL AUTOBOTS

We have a Transformers toy bundle to give away!

If you want to be in with a chance to receive this
awesome prize just answer this question:

WHAT KIND OF DECEPTICON
IS THUNDERHOOF?

Write your answer on the back of a postcard and send it to:
Transformers Competition
Hachette Children's Group
Carmelite House, 50 Victoria Embankment
London, EC4Y 0DZ

Closing Date: December 2nd 2016

For full terms and conditions go to www.hachettechildrens.co.uk/terms

THE ALL-NEW ACTION-PACKED ADVENTURES

OUT NOW ON DVD & DIGITAL HD